Original illustrations and design by Fine™

Library of Congress Cataloging-in-Publication Data

Fine.
French kitty goes to Paris / written and illustrated by Fine.
p. cm.
Summary: A fashionable feline named Kitty packs her bags and goes to Paris for a weekend.
ISBN 0-8109-4447-2
[1. Cats—Fiction. 2. Paris (France)—Fiction. 3. France—Fiction.] I. Title.

PZ7.F4956667 Fr 2003
[E]—dc21

2002151832

For more fashion-packed adventures with French Kitty® and her friends, please visit:

www.welovefine.com

Published in 2003 by Harry N. Abrams, Incorporated, New York

Printed and bound in China
10 9 8 7 6 5 4 3 2 1

Harry N. Abrams, Inc.
100 Fifth Avenue
New York, N.Y. 10011
www.abramsbooks.com

Abrams is a subsidiary of
LA MARTINIÈRE
GROUPE

Kitty Goes to Paris

Featuring French Kitty® by Fine™

Harry N. Abrams, Inc., Publishers

pour Natalie

One Friday morning
while having a chat,
Kitty said, "Birdie,
let's buy a new hat!"

The time to go shopping
was that very day.
Off to Paris they flew.
No time for delay!

Miss Kitty Fine

USA

UNITED STATES OF AM

PASSPORT

Surname
FINE

Given names
KITTY KAT

Nationality
UNITED STATES OF AM

Sex F Date of birth 01/JA

Place of birth NEW YORK

"Bon voyage!"

Yes, to Paris in France
to see the real

Couture

(meaning "high fashion" in French,
of this Kitty was sure).

"Bon appétit!"

When they got to Paris

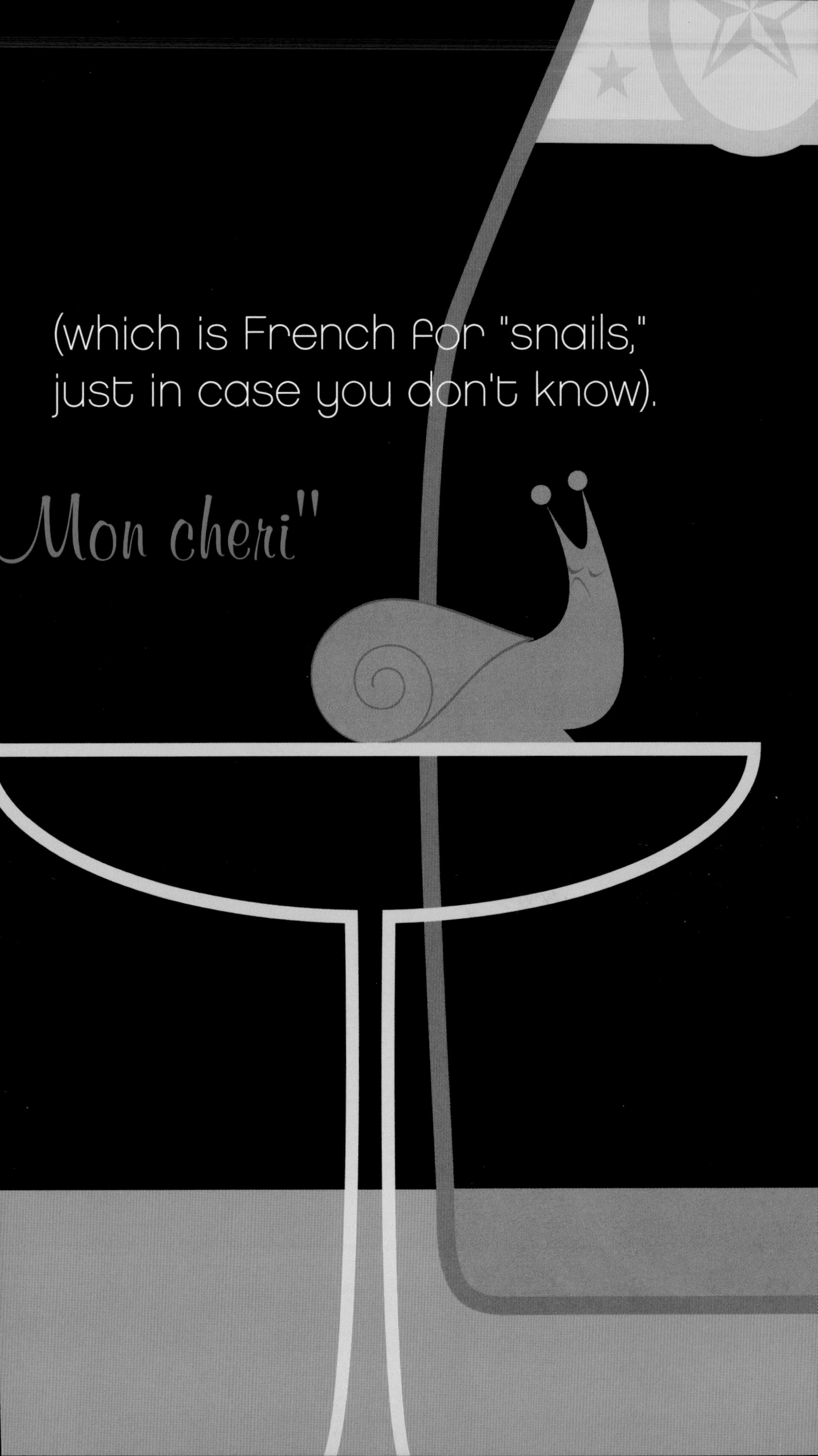
(which is French for "snails,"
just in case you don't know).
Mon cheri"

Haute
Couture

Their very next stop was the chic Hautiepuss Salon for manicures, pedicures and so forth and so on.

After that they went to
Monsieur FiFi LaFoo's,
the creator of hats

custom-made just for you.

His hats were unique
with pizzazz and with flair.
How would Kitty choose?
Life is just so unfair!

"Gaucho-cho"
"Je ne sais pas!"
Hong Kong Garden"

"Party Clown"
"Très chic!"
"Schoolboy"

Then confusion took over
and chaos reigned supreme.
Kitty began to feel faint
as she heard FiFi scream...

"This one's extra sassy!
It suits you. That's that!"
Kitty sighed with relief.
Birdie, too, loved the hat.

"Oui! Oui!"

So Kitty thanked FiFi
and went on her way
with Birdie through Paris
to enjoy the day.

Merci beaucoup!

They paused for a rest
at a sweet sidewalk café,
where an artist insisted
she pose right away!

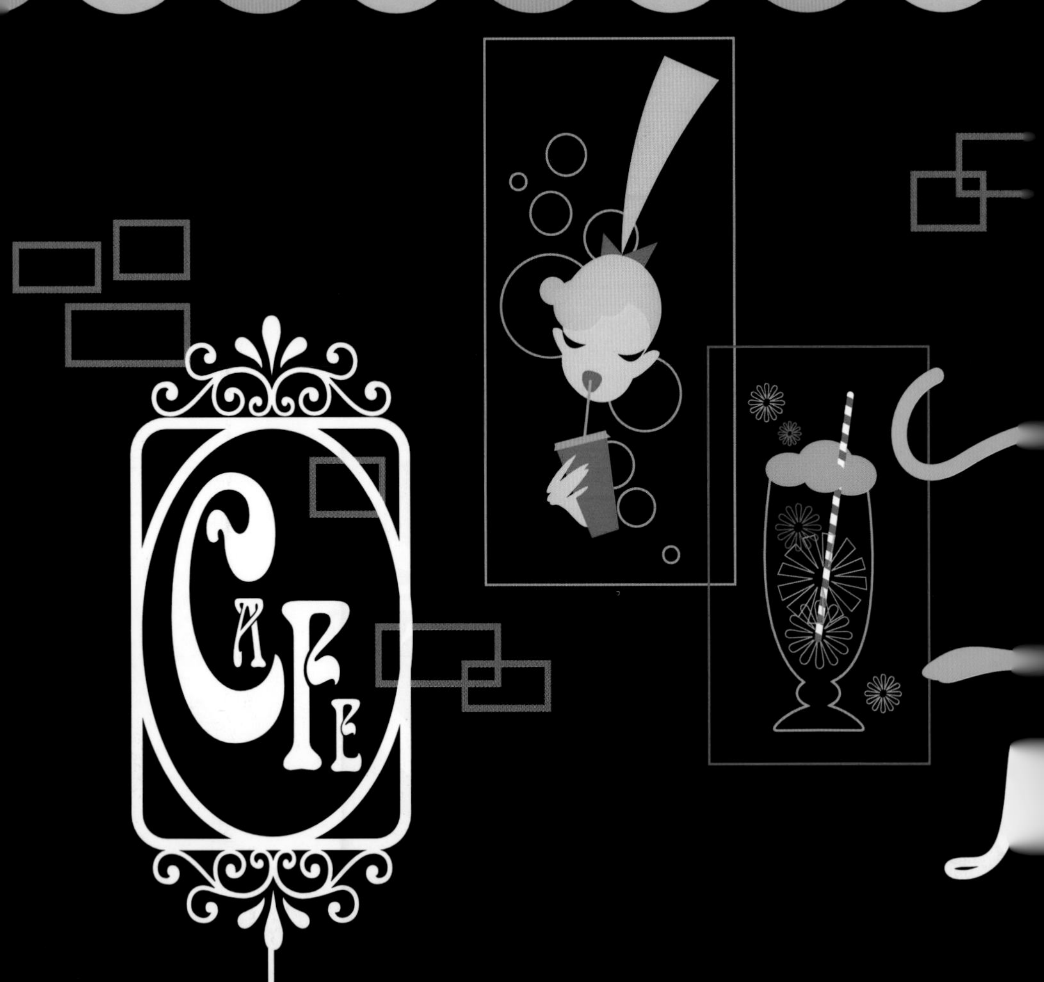

"S'il vous plaît?"

"Jean DuChat is my name,
and for Mademoiselle Kitty,
this portrait, a small souvenir
of my lovely city."

"Oh la la!"
Du Chat

With the painting complete there was still time to spare

"Très vite!"
for
quick
scooter
ride
through
the
city

"Au revoir"

They saw all of Paris
in under an hour
then said their good-byes
near the Eiffel Tower.

Kitty's hat-shopping spree
had been such a success,

they happily flew home
to their New York address.

Du Chat

Birdie was just thrilled
by the haute couture hat.
Kitty loved Paris...

and that really was that!

French Glossary

Chapeau –Hat

Bon voyage –Have a great trip

Bon appétit –Enjoy your meal

Mon cheri –My love

Je ne sais pas –I don't know

Très chic –Very chic

Magnifique –Magnificent

Oui! Oui! –Yes! Yes!

Merci beaucoup –Thank you very muc

S'il vous plaît –Please

Oh la la –Oh la la

Très vite –Very fast

Au revoir –Good-bye

Vive Paris –Long live Paris

and Tout va bien means

Everything's Fine

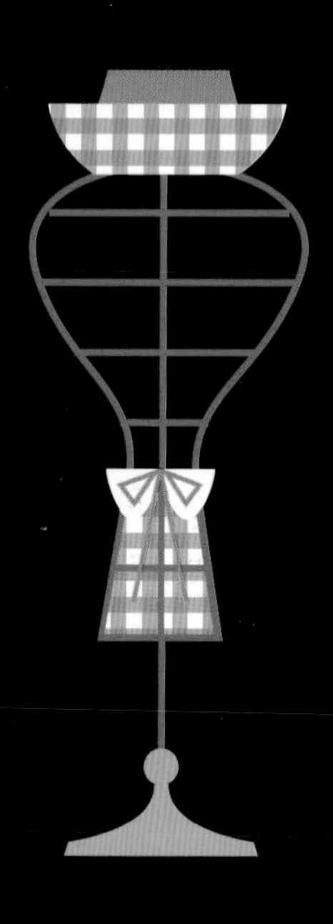